Dirt

by Luana K. Mitten and

Contents

Where is Dirt Found? . . .2
What is Dirt Made From? 4
What Lives in Dirt? 8
How Dirt Moves 12
Taking Care of Dirt 16

ROURKE CLASSROOM RESOURCES
The path to student success

Where is Dirt Found?

Dirt, mud, soil... No matter what you call it, all living things depend on it.

 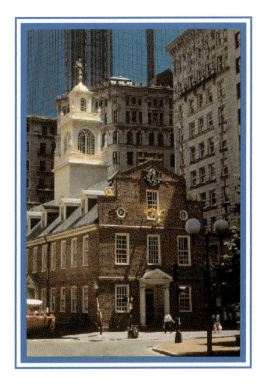

We can see dirt on some parts of the Earth. But most dirt is hidden under plants and buildings.

What is Dirt Made From?

Dirt is a **mixture** of topsoil, sand, clay, and rocks.

The part of dirt that feels soft and wet is topsoil. It is made when dead plants and animals rot.

The part of dirt that feels grainy is sand.

The parts of dirt that feel hard are rocks and clay. Clay will **crumble** but rocks will not.

What Lives in Dirt?

Many bugs live in the dirt. They eat dead plants and animals. Their droppings **enrich** the soil.

Earthworms live in the dirt. They **aerate** the soil by wiggling and tunneling through it.

Moles and snakes live in the dirt.

Larger animals build burrows and dens in the dirt.

How Dirt Moves

Heavy rains or rivers can carry dirt away from fields and plant roots. We call that erosion.

We use tools and machines to move dirt.

Dirt, mud, soil... We can't live without it. All living things on our planet depend on dirt.

Taking Care of Dirt

You can help to take care of the Earth's dirt. Which things belong in dirt? Which things don't?